THE AMATEUR

RICHARD HARDING DAVIS

The Amateur
By Richard Harding Davis
Annotated Edition

Printed in the United States of America
First Edition: July 2025

CONTENTS

FOREWORD

Some stories don't arrive with fanfare. They sidle in, take a seat, and let your attention catch up to them. The Amateur is one of those—quiet on the surface, steady underneath, and suddenly personal before you realize what's happened.

Richard Harding Davis knew spectacle. He covered wars, traveled with armies, and turned the front lines into front-page prose. Yet here he chooses another register. Instead of artillery, there's conversation; instead of open battle, a sharp turn from watching to doing. The tension lives in that hinge—how an onlooker becomes a participant, and what it costs to cross the line.

London makes a fitting stage. Not the postcard city of fog alone, but a lived-in metropolis of hotel lounges, bars, and taxicabs, where small hesitations matter: a pause at a coatroom door, a greeting aimed a beat too confidently, a glance that lasts a fraction too long. Davis writes as someone who notices the seams—the way places hold their breath when no one is supposed to be looking. Ambiguity suits this London, and this story.

What hooks you is less the machinery of detection than the pressure of feeling. The hero, Austin Ford, is no virtuoso sleuth. He is, as advertised, an amateur—quick-eyed, bold enough, and still prone to misread what's in front of him. That lack of polish is the point. When he misjudges a situation or steps in on nerve and guesswork, the narrative gains its charge. We sense the stakes not because the world is ending, but because one choice can upend several lives.

Davis resists the easy satisfactions of a clockwork mystery. He's after something slipperier: the ethics and hazards of involvement. When do you stop taking notes and raise a hand? What debt do you incur when you act on someone else's story? Here those questions take shape in a hunt that tangles with con games, decoys, and mistaken identity—and in the unsettling discovery that good intentions can be used as bait. Not everything resolves; enough does.

It matters that the protagonist is a journalist. Davis knew that vantage—the habit of hanging back, of turning life into copy. The Amateur tests that posture. Curiosity, once it warms into care, asks for more than observation. The pursuit here isn't glory. It's clarity, maybe connection, and the price of both.

A gentle loneliness threads the novella. Not grand isolation, but the traveler's ache: the sense of moving through other people's settled lives with your suitcase still in hand. Davis gives side characters weight without overexplaining them. We hear what is not said, and quiet scenes—a ship's corridor, a hotel lounge, the close dark of a taxi—do the heavy lifting.

The style is lean. Davis trusts the unsaid, avoids ornament, and lets timing do what rhetoric can't. In an era fond of bangs and sparkles, the restraint feels bracing. A single withheld line lands harder than a speech.

For first-time readers of Davis, this is a fine beginning—compact without feeling slight, lucid without slipping into sentiment. For longtime admirers, it shows a different facet: introspection from a writer famous for motion. The reporter who usually stands outside the frame steps one pace forward.

This edition includes a brief biography to situate the man behind the sentences. Davis was a bundle of contradictions—dapper and daring, worldly and tender—and those tensions thread his fiction. They help explain why this story, more than a century on, still feels alert to human risk.

A BRIEF BIOGRAPHY

Richard Harding Davis didn't just write stories—he chased them down alleys in war-torn cities, smoked them over midnight drinks with diplomats, and sometimes wore them like a tailored suit. He was the kind of man who could file a dispatch from the front lines in Cuba, then turn around and write a novella that read like a cocktail of wit, charm, and danger.

Born in 1864 in Philadelphia, Davis grew up in a house where words mattered. His mother, Rebecca Harding Davis, was a literary force in her own right—one of the first American writers to tackle social injustice head-on. She wrote about factory workers and poverty while most of her peers were still writing about tea parties. Richard inherited her fire, but he added his own flair: a taste for adventure, a love of style, and a knack for storytelling that could make even a telegram feel like a page-turner.

He wasn't a model student. He attended Lehigh University and later Johns Hopkins, but classrooms couldn't hold him for long. What he needed was a train ticket, a notebook, and something worth chasing. By his twenties, he was already making a name at big-city papers—and soon after became a managing editor at Harper's Weekly—and by thirty he was covering wars in Cuba and South Africa, with later reporting from the Russo-Japanese War and World War I.

Davis didn't just report—he performed. He showed up to battlefields with a distinctive sense of style, a journalist who looked like he meant business. During World War I, on the Salonika front, he was even arrested as a suspected spy and then released. In Cuba, his vivid coverage of Theodore Roosevelt and the Rough Riders helped forge their legend, and he was made an honorary member. His writing was fast, vivid, and cinematic—he made readers feel the heat, hear the gunfire, and smell the cigar smoke.

But he wasn't all war and bravado. Davis had a softer side, too. He wrote fiction that explored identity, romance, and the strange ways people deceive themselves and each other. The Amateur is one of those stories—a novella about a journalist who gets tangled in a mystery that's as emotional as it is criminal. It's not just about solving a puzzle; it's about what happens when you stop watching and start feeling. That tension between observer and participant was something Davis knew intimately.

He was a romantic, but not naïve. He married twice—first to artist Cecil Clark, and later to Bessie McCoy, a vaudeville star known for her high-kicking "Yama Yama Man." They were a glamorous pair—he, the globe-trotting writer; she, the stage sensation. Their life together was a whirlwind of parties, travel, and creative energy.

Davis was also obsessed with appearances—not just in fashion, but in how people presented themselves to the world. He believed in honor, style, and the idea that a man should look ready for anything. His influence even helped popularize the clean-shaven look at the turn of the century. That ethos shows up in his characters, who are often polished on the outside but wrestling with something deeper underneath.

He died young—just 51—after a heart attack in New York City, while on the telephone. At the time, he was one of the most famous writers in America. Today, he's less known, but his work still crackles with energy. His stories aren't dusty relics; they're snapshots of a man who lived fast, wrote hard, and never stopped chasing the next headline.

If you're reading The Amateur, you're stepping into Davis's world—a place where mystery meets emotion, and where even the most polished characters have something messy lurking beneath the surface. It's not just a story. It's a glimpse into the mind of a man who believed that life was best lived with a pen in one hand and a passport in the other.

THE AMATEUR

I

It was February off the Banks, and so thick was the weather that, on the upper decks, one could have driven a sleigh. Inside the smoking-room Austin Ford, as securely sheltered from the blizzard as though he had been sitting in front of a wood fire at his club, ordered hot gin for himself and the ship's doctor. The ship's doctor had gone below on another "hurry call" from the widow. At the first luncheon on board the widow had sat on the right of Doctor Sparrow, with Austin Ford facing her. But since then, except to the doctor, she had been invisible. So, at frequent intervals, the ill health of the widow had deprived Ford of the society of the doctor. That it deprived him, also, of the society of the widow did not concern him. HER life had not been spent upon ocean liners; she could not remember when state-rooms were named after the States of the Union. She could not tell him of shipwrecks and salvage, of smugglers and of the modern pirates who found their victims in the smoking-room.

Ford was on his way to England to act as the London correspondent of the New York Republic.

For three years on that most sensational of the New York dailies he had been the star man, the chief muckraker, the chief sleuth. His interest was in crime. Not in crimes committed in passion or inspired by drink, but in such offences against law and society as are perpetrated with nice intelligence. The murderer, the burglar, the strong-arm men who, in side streets, waylay respectable citizens did not appeal to him. The man he studied, pursued, and exposed was the cashier who evolved a new method of covering up his peculations, the dishonest president of an insurance company, the confidence man who used no concealed weapon other than his wit. Toward the criminals he pursued young Ford felt no personal animosity. He harassed them as he would have shot a hawk killing chickens. Not because he disliked the hawk, but because the battle was unequal, and because he felt sorry for the chickens.

Had you called Austin Ford an amateur detective he would have been greatly annoyed. He argued that his position was similar to that of the dramatic critic. The dramatic critic warned the public against bad plays; Ford warned it against bad men. Having done that, he left it to the public to determine whether the bad man should thrive or perish.

When the managing editor told him of his appointment to London, Ford had protested that his work lay in New York; that of London and the English, except as a tourist and sight-seer, he knew nothing.

"That's just why we are sending you," explained the managing editor. "Our readers are ignorant. To make them read about London you've got to tell them about themselves in London. They like to know who's been presented at court, about the American girls who have married dukes; and which ones opened a bazaar, and which one opened a hat shop, and which is getting a divorce. Don't send us anything concerning suffragettes and Dreadnaughts. Just send us stuff about Americans. If you take your meals in the Carlton grill-room and drink at the Cecil you can pick up more good stories than we can print. You will find lots of your friends over there. Some of those girls who married dukes," he suggested, "know you, don't they?"

"Not since they married dukes," said Ford.

"Well, anyway, all your other friends will be there," continued the managing editor encouragingly. "Now that they have shut up the tracks here all the con men have gone to London. They say an American can't take a drink at the Salisbury without his fellow-countrymen having a fight as to which one will sell him a gold brick."

Ford's eyes lightened in pleasurable anticipation.

"Look them over," urged the managing editor, "and send us a special. Call it 'The American Invasion.' Don't you see a story in it?"

"It will be the first one I send you," said Ford. The ship's doctor returned from his visit below decks and sank into the leather cushion close to Ford's elbow. For a few moments the older man sipped doubtfully at his gin and water, and, as though perplexed, rubbed his hand over his bald and shining head. "I told her to talk to you," he said fretfully.

"Her? Who?" inquired Ford. "Oh, the widow?"

"You were right about that," said Doctor Sparrow; "she is not a widow."

The reporter smiled complacently.

"Do you know why I thought not?" he demanded. "Because all the time she was at luncheon she kept turning over her wedding-ring as though she was not used to it. It was a new ring, too. I told you then she was not a widow."

"Do you always notice things like that?" asked the doctor.

"Not on purpose," said the amateur detective; "I can't help it. I see ten things where other people see only one; just as some men run ten times as fast as other men. We have tried it out often at the office; put all sorts of junk under a newspaper, lifted the newspaper for five seconds, and then each man wrote down what he had seen. Out of twenty things I would remember seventeen. The next best guess would be about nine. Once I saw a man lift his coat collar to hide his face. It was in the Grand Central Station. I stopped him, and told him he was wanted. Turned out he WAS wanted. It was Goldberg, making his getaway to Canada."

"It is a gift," said the doctor.

"No, it's a nuisance," laughed the reporter. "I see so many things I don't want to see. I see that people are wearing clothes that are not made for them. I see when women are lying to me. I can see when men are on the verge of a nervous breakdown, and whether it is drink or debt or morphine—"

The doctor snorted triumphantly.

"You did not see that the widow was on the verge of a breakdown!"

"No," returned the reporter. "Is she? I'm sorry."

"If you're sorry," urged the doctor eagerly, "you'll help her. She is going to London alone to find her husband. He has disappeared. She thinks that he has been murdered, or that he is lying ill in some hospital. I told her if any one could help her to find him you could. I had to say something. She's very ill."

"To find her husband in London?" repeated Ford. "London is a large town."

"She has photographs of him and she knows where he spends his time," pleaded the doctor. "He is a company promoter. It should be easy for you."

"Maybe he doesn't want her to find him," said Ford. "Then it wouldn't be so easy for me."

The old doctor sighed heavily. "I know," he murmured. "I thought of that, too. And she is so very pretty."

"That was another thing I noticed," said Ford.

The doctor gave no heed.

"She must stop worrying," he exclaimed, "or she will have a mental collapse. I have tried sedatives, but they don't touch her. I want to give her courage. She is frightened. She's left a baby boy at home, and she's fearful that something will happen to him, and she's frightened at being at sea, frightened at being alone in London; it's pitiful." The old man shook his head. "Pitiful! Will you talk to her now?" he asked.

"Nonsense!" exclaimed Ford. "She doesn't want to tell the story of her life to strange young men."

"But it was she suggested it," cried the doctor. "She asked me if you were Austin Ford, the great detective."

Ford snorted scornfully. "She did not!" he protested. His tone was that of a man who hopes to be contradicted.

"But she did," insisted the doctor, "and I told her your specialty was tracing persons. Her face lightened at once; it gave her hope. She will listen to you. Speak very gently and kindly and confidently. Say you are sure you can find him."

"Where is the lady now?" asked Ford.

Doctor Sparrow scrambled eagerly to his feet. "She cannot leave her cabin," he answered.

The widow, as Ford and Doctor Sparrow still thought of her, was lying on the sofa that ran the length of the state-room, parallel with the lower berth. She was fully dressed, except that instead of her bodice she wore a kimono that left her throat and arms bare. She had been sleeping, and when their entrance awoke her, her blue eyes regarded them uncomprehendingly. Ford, hidden from her by the doctor, observed that not only was she very pretty, but that she was absurdly young, and that the drowsy smile she turned upon the old man before she noted the presence of Ford was as innocent as that of a baby. Her cheeks were flushed, her eyes brilliant, her yellow curls had become loosened and were spread upon the pillow. When she saw Ford she caught the kimono so closely around her throat that she choked. Had the doctor not pushed her down she would have stood.

"I thought," she stammered, "he was an OLD man."

The doctor, misunderstanding, hastened to reassure her. "Mr. Ford is old in experience," he said soothingly. "He has had remarkable success. Why, he found a criminal once just because the man wore a collar. And he found Walsh, the burglar, and Phillips, the forger, and a gang of counterfeiters—"

Mrs. Ashton turned upon him, her eyes wide with wonder. "But MY husband," she protested, "is not a criminal!"

"My dear lady!" the doctor cried. "I did not mean that, of course not. I meant, if Mr. Ford can find men who don't wish to be found, how easy for him to find a man who—" He turned helplessly to Ford. "You tell her," he begged.

Ford sat down on a steamer trunk that protruded from beneath the berth, and, turning to the widow, gave her the full benefit of his working smile. It was confiding, helpless, appealing. It showed a trustfulness in the person to whom it was addressed that caused that individual to believe Ford needed protection from a wicked world.

"Doctor Sparrow tells me," began Ford timidly, "you have lost your husband's address; that you will let me try to find him. If I can help in any way I should be glad."

The young girl regarded him, apparently, with disappointment. It was as though Doctor Sparrow had led her to expect a man full of years and authority, a man upon whom she could lean; not a youth whose smile seemed to beg one not to scold him. She gave Ford three photographs, bound together with a string.

"When Doctor Sparrow told me you could help me I got out these," she said.

Ford jotted down a mental note to the effect that she "got them out." That is, she did not keep them where she could always look at them. That she was not used to look at them was evident by the fact that they were bound together.

The first photograph showed three men standing in an open place and leaning on a railing. One of them was smiling toward the photographer. He was a good-looking young man of about thirty years of age, well fed, well dressed, and apparently well satisfied with the world and himself. Ford's own smile had disappeared. His eyes were alert and interested.

"The one with the Panama hat pulled down over his eyes is your husband?" he asked.

"Yes," assented the widow. Her tone showed slight surprise.

"This was taken about a year ago?" inquired Ford. "Must have been," he answered himself; "they haven't raced at the Bay since then. This was taken in front of the club stand—probably for the Telegraph?" He lifted his eyes inquiringly.

Rising on her elbow the young wife bent forward toward the photograph. "Does it say that there," she asked doubtfully. "How did you guess that?"

In his role as chorus the ship's doctor exclaimed with enthusiasm: "Didn't I tell you? He's wonderful."

Ford cut him off impatiently. "You never saw a rail as high as that except around a racetrack," he muttered. "And the badge in his buttonhole and the angle of the stand all show—"

He interrupted himself to address the widow. "This is an owner's badge. What was the name of his stable?"

"I don't know," she answered. She regarded the young man with sudden uneasiness. "They only owned one horse, but I believe that gave them the privilege of—"

"I see," exclaimed Ford. "Your husband is a bookmaker. But in London he is a promoter of companies."

"So my friend tells me," said Mrs. Ashton. "She's just got back from London. Her husband told her that Harry, my husband, was always at the American bar in the Cecil or at the Salisbury or the Savoy." The girl shook her head. "But a woman can't go looking for a man there," she protested. "That's why I thought you—"

"That'll be all right," Ford assured her hurriedly. "It's a coincidence, but it happens that my own work takes me to these hotels, and if your husband is there I will find him." He returned the photographs.

"Hadn't you better keep one?" she asked.

"I won't forget him," said the reporter. "Besides"—he turned his eyes toward the doctor and, as though thinking aloud, said—"he may have grown a beard."

There was a pause.

The eyes of the woman grew troubled. Her lips pressed together as though in a sudden access of pain.

"And he may," Ford continued, "have changed his name."

As though fearful, if she spoke, the tears would fall, the girl nodded her head stiffly.

Having learned what he wanted to know Ford applied to the wound a soothing ointment of promises and encouragement.

"He's as good as found," he protested. "You will see him in a day, two days after you land."

The girl's eyes opened happily. She clasped her hands together and raised them.

"You will try?" she begged. "You will find him for me"—she corrected herself eagerly—"for me and the baby?"

The loose sleeves of the kimono fell back to her shoulders showing the white arms; the eyes raised to Ford were glistening with tears.

"Of course I will find him," growled the reporter.

He freed himself from the appeal in the eyes of the young mother and left the cabin. The doctor followed. He was bubbling over with enthusiasm.

"That was fine!" he cried. "You said just the right thing. There will be no collapse now."

His satisfaction was swept away in a burst of disgust.

"The blackguard!" he protested. "To desert a wife as young as that and as pretty as that."

"So I have been thinking," said the reporter. "I guess," he added gravely, "what is going to happen is that before I find her husband I will have got to know him pretty well."

Apparently, young Mrs. Ashton believed everything would come to pass just as Ford promised it would and as he chose to order it; for the next day, with a color not born of fever in her cheeks and courage in her eyes, she joined Ford and the doctor at the luncheon-table. Her attention was concentrated on the younger man. In him she saw the one person who could bring her husband to her.

"She acts," growled the doctor later in the smoking-room, "as though she was afraid you were going to back out of your promise and jump overboard."

"Don't think," he protested violently, "it's you she's interested in. All she sees in you is what you can do for her. Can you see that?"

"Any one as clever at seeing things as I am," returned the reporter, "cannot help but see that."

Later, as Ford was walking on the upper deck, Mrs. Ashton came toward him, beating her way against the wind. Without a trace of coquetry or self-consciousness, and with a sigh of content, she laid her hand on his arm.

"When I don't see you," she exclaimed as simply as a child, "I feel so frightened. When I see you I know all will come right. Do you mind if I walk with you?" she asked. "And do you mind if every now and then I ask you to tell me again it will all come right?"

For the three days following Mrs. Ashton and Ford were constantly together. Or, at least, Mrs. Ashton was constantly with Ford. She told him that when she sat in her cabin the old fears returned to her, and in these moments of panic she searched the ship for him.

The doctor protested that he was growing jealous.

"I'm not so greatly to be envied," suggested Ford. "'Harry' at meals three times a day and on deck all the rest of the day becomes monotonous. On a closer acquaintance with Harry he seems to be a decent sort of a young man; at least he seems to have been at one time very much in love with her."

"Well," sighed the doctor sentimentally, "she is certainly very much in love with Harry."

Ford shook his head non-committingly. "I don't know her story," he said. "Don't want to know it."

The ship was in the channel, on her way to Cherbourg, and running as smoothly as a clock.

From the shore friendly lights told them they were nearing their journey's end; that the land was on every side. Seated on a steamer-chair next to his in the semi-darkness of the deck, Mrs. Ashton began to talk nervously and eagerly.

"Now that we are so near," she murmured, "I have got to tell you something. If you did not know I would feel I had not been fair. You might think that when you were doing so much for me I should have been more honest."

She drew a long breath. "It's so hard," she said.

"Wait," commanded Ford. "Is it going to help me to find him?"

"No."

"Then don't tell me."

His tone caused the girl to start. She leaned toward him and peered into his face. His eyes, as he looked back to her, were kind and comprehending.

"You mean," said the amateur detective, "that your husband has deserted you. That if it were not for the baby you would not try to find him. Is that it?"

Mrs. Ashton breathed quickly and turned her face away.

"Yes," she whispered. "That is it."

There was a long pause. When she faced him again the fact that there was no longer a secret between them seemed to give her courage.

"Maybe," she said, "you can understand. Maybe you can tell me what it means. I have thought and thought. I have gone over it and over it until when I go back to it my head aches. I have done nothing else but think, and I can't make it seem better. I can't find any excuse. I have had no one to talk to, no one I could tell. I have thought maybe a man could understand." She raised her eyes appealingly.

"If you can only make it seem less cruel. Don't you see," she cried miserably, "I want to believe; I want to forgive him. I want to think he loves me. Oh! I want so to be able to love him; but how can I? I can't! I can't!"

In the week in which they had been thrown together the girl unconsciously had told Ford much about herself and her husband. What she now told him was but an amplification of what he had guessed.

She had met Ashton a year and a half before, when she had just left school at the convent and had returned to live with her family. Her home was at Far Rockaway. Her father was a cashier in a bank at Long Island City. One night, with a party of friends, she had been taken to a dance at one of the beach hotels, and there met Ashton. At that time he was one of a firm that was making book at the Aqueduct race-track. The girl had met very few men and with them was shy and frightened, but with Ashton she found herself at once at ease. That night he drove her and her friends home in his touring-car and the next day they teased her about her conquest. It made her very happy. After that she went to hops at the hotel, and as the bookmaker did not dance, the two young people sat upon the piazza. Then Ashton came to see her at her own house, but when her father learned that the young man who had been calling upon her was a bookmaker he told him he could not associate with his daughter.

But the girl was now deeply in love with Ashton, and apparently he with her. He begged her to marry him. They knew that to this, partly from prejudice and partly owing to his position in the bank, her father would object. Accordingly they agreed that in August, when the racing moved to Saratoga, they would run away and get married at that place. Their plan was that Ashton would leave for Saratoga with the other racing men, and that she would join him the next day.

They had arranged to be married by a magistrate, and Ashton had shown her a letter from one at

Saratoga who consented to perform the ceremony. He had given her an engagement ring and two thousand dollars, which he asked her to keep for him, lest tempted at the track he should lose it.

But she assured Ford it was not such material things as a letter, a ring, or gift of money that had led her to trust Ashton. His fear of losing her, his complete subjection to her wishes, his happiness in her presence, all seemed to prove that to make her happy was his one wish, and that he could do anything to make her unhappy appeared impossible.

They were married the morning she arrived at Saratoga; and the same day departed for Niagara Falls and Quebec. The honeymoon lasted ten days. They were ten days of complete happiness. No one, so the girl declared, could have been more kind, more unselfishly considerate than her husband. They returned to Saratoga and engaged a suite of rooms at one of the big hotels. Ashton was not satisfied with the rooms shown him, and leaving her upstairs returned to the office floor to ask for others.

Since that moment his wife had never seen him nor heard from him.

On the day of her marriage young Mrs. Ashton had written to her father, asking him to give her his good wishes and pardon. He refused both. As she had feared, he did not consider that for a bank clerk a gambler made a desirable son-in-law; and the letters he wrote his daughter were so bitter that in reply she informed him he had forced her to choose between her family and her husband, and that she chose her husband. In consequence, when she found herself deserted she felt she could not return to her people. She remained in Saratoga. There she moved into cheap lodgings, and in order that the two thousand dollars Ashton had left with her might be saved for his child, she had learned to type-write, and after four months had been able to support herself. Within the last month a girl friend, who had known both Ashton and herself before they were married, had written her that her husband was living in London. For the sake of her son she had at once determined to make an effort to seek him out.

"The son, nonsense!" exclaimed the doctor, when Ford retold the story. "She is not crossing the ocean because she is worried about the future of her son. She seeks her own happiness. The woman is in love with her husband."

Ford shook his head.

"I don't know!" he objected. "She's so extravagant in her praise of Harry that it seems unreal. It sounds insincere. Then, again, when I swear I will find him she shows a delight that you might describe as savage, almost vindictive. As though, if I did find Harry, the first thing she would do would be to stick a knife in him."

"Maybe," volunteered the doctor sadly, "she has heard there is a woman in the case. Maybe she is the one she's thinking of sticking the knife into?"

"Well," declared the reporter, "if she doesn't stop looking savage every time I promise to find Harry I won't find Harry. Why should I act the part of Fate, anyway? How do I know that Harry hasn't got a wife in London and several in the States? How do we know he didn't leave his country for his country's good? That's what it looks like to me. How can we tell what confronted him the day he went down to the hotel desk to change his rooms and, instead, got into his touring-car and beat the speed limit to Canada. Whom did he meet in the hotel corridor? A woman with a perfectly good marriage certificate, or a detective with a perfectly good warrant? Or did Harry find out that his bride had a devil of a temper of her own, and that for him marriage was a failure? The widow is certainly a very charming young woman, but there may be two sides to this."

"You are a cynic, sir," protested the doctor.

"That may be," growled the reporter, "but I am not a private detective agency, or a matrimonial bureau, and before I hear myself saying, 'Bless you, my children!' both of these young people will have to show me why they should not be kept asunder."

II

On the afternoon of their arrival in London Ford convoyed Mrs. Ashton to an old-established private hotel in Craven Street.

"Here," he explained, "you will be within a few hundred yards of the place in which your husband is said to spend his time. I will be living in the same hotel. If I find him you will know it in ten minutes."

The widow gave a little gasp, whether of excitement or of happiness Ford could not determine.

"Whatever happens," she begged, "will you let me hear from you sometimes? You are the only person I know in London—and—it's so big it frightens me. I don't want to be a burden," she went on eagerly, "but if I can feel you are within call—"

"What you need," said Ford heartily, "is less of the doctor's nerve tonic and sleeping draughts, and a little innocent diversion. To-night I am going to take you to the Savoy to supper."

Mrs. Ashton exclaimed delightedly, and then was filled with misgivings.

"I have nothing to wear," she protested, "and over here, in the evening, the women dress so well. I have a dinner gown," she exclaimed, "but it's black. Would that do?"

Ford assured her nothing could be better. He had a man's vanity in liking a woman with whom he was seen in public to be pretty and smartly dressed, and he felt sure that in black the blond beauty of Mrs. Ashton would appear to advantage. They arranged to meet at eleven on the promenade leading to the Savoy supper-room, and parted with mutual satisfaction at the prospect.

The finding of Harry Ashton was so simple that in its very simplicity it appeared spectacular.

On leaving Mrs. Ashton, Ford engaged rooms at the Hotel Cecil. Before visiting his rooms he made his way to the American bar. He did not go there seeking Harry Ashton. His object was entirely self-centred. His purpose was to drink to himself and to the lights of London. But as though by appointment, the man he had promised to find was waiting for him. As Ford entered the room, at a table facing the door sat Ashton. There was no mistaking him. He wore a mustache, but it was no disguise. He was the same good-natured, good-looking youth who, in the photograph from under a Panama hat, had smiled upon the world. With a glad cry Ford rushed toward him.

"Fancy meeting YOU!" he exclaimed.

Mr. Ashton's good-natured smile did not relax. He merely shook his head.

"Afraid you have made a mistake," he said. The reporter regarded him blankly. His face showed his disappointment.

"Aren't you Charles W. Garrett, of New York?" he demanded.

"Not me," said Mr. Ashton.

"But," Ford insisted in hurt tones, as though he were being trifled with, "you have been told you look like him, haven't you?"

Mr. Ashton's good nature was unassailable.

"Sorry," he declared, "never heard of him."

Ford became garrulous, he could not believe two men could look so much alike. It was a remarkable coincidence. The stranger must certainly have a drink, the drink intended for his twin. Ashton was bored, but accepted. He was well acquainted with the easy good-fellowship of his countrymen. The room in which he sat was a meeting-place for them. He considered that they were always giving each other drinks, and not only were they always introducing themselves, but saying, "Shake hands with my friend, Mr. So-and-So." After five minutes they showed each other photographs of the children. This one, though as loquacious as the others, seemed better dressed, more "wise"; he brought to the exile the atmosphere of his beloved Broadway, so Ashton drank to him pleasantly.

"My name is Sydney Carter," he volunteered.

As a poker-player skims over the cards in his hand, Ford, in his mind's eye, ran over the value of giving or not giving his right name. He decided that Ashton would not have heard it and that, if he gave a false one, there was a chance that later Ashton might find out that he had done so. Accordingly he said, "Mine is Austin Ford," and seated himself at Ashton's table. Within ten minutes the man he had promised to pluck from among the eight million inhabitants of London was smiling sympathetically at his jests and buying a drink.

On the steamer Ford had rehearsed the story with which, should he meet Ashton, he would introduce himself. It was one arranged to fit with his theory that Ashton was a crook. If Ashton were a crook Ford argued that to at once ingratiate himself in his good graces he also must be a crook. His plan was to invite Ashton to co-operate with him in some scheme that was openly dishonest. By so doing he hoped apparently to place himself at

Ashton's mercy. He believed if he could persuade Ashton he was more of a rascal than Ashton himself, and an exceedingly stupid rascal, any distrust the bookmaker might feel toward him would disappear. He made his advances so openly, and apparently showed his hand so carelessly, that, from being bored, Ashton became puzzled, then interested; and when Ford insisted he should dine with him, he considered it so necessary to find out who the youth might be who was forcing himself upon him that he accepted the invitation.

They adjourned to dress and an hour later, at Ford's suggestion, they met at the Carlton. There Ford ordered a dinner calculated to lull his newly made friend into a mood suited to confidence, but which had on Ashton exactly the opposite effect. Merely for the pleasure of his company, utter strangers were not in the habit of treating him to strawberries in February, and vintage champagne; and, in consequence, in Ford's hospitality he saw only cause for suspicion. If, as he had first feared, Ford was a New York detective, it was most important he should know that. No one better than Ashton understood that, at that moment, his presence in New York meant, for the police, unalloyed satisfaction, and for himself undisturbed solitude. But Ford was unlike any detective of his acquaintance; and his acquaintance had been extensive. It was true Ford was familiar with all the habits of Broadway and the Tenderloin. Of places with which Ashton was intimate, and of men with whom Ashton had formerly been well acquainted, he talked glibly. But, if he were a detective, Ashton considered, they certainly had improved the class.

The restaurant into which for the first time Ashton had penetrated, and in which he felt ill at ease, was to Ford, he observed, a matter of course. Evidently for Ford it held no terrors. He criticised the service, patronized the head waiters, and grumbled at the food; and when, on leaving the restaurant, an Englishman and his wife stopped at their table to greet him, he accepted their welcome to London without embarrassment.

Ashton, rolling his cigar between his lips, observed the incident with increasing bewilderment.

"You've got some swell friends," he growled. "I'll bet you never met THEM at Healey's!"

"I meet all kinds of people in my business," said Ford. "I once sold that man some mining stock, and the joke of it was," he added, smiling knowingly, "it turned out to be good."

Ashton decided that the psychological moment had arrived.

"What IS your business?" he asked.

"I'm a company promoter," said Ford easily. "I thought I told you."

"I did not tell you that I was a company promoter, too, did I?" demanded Ashton.

"No," answered Ford, with apparent surprise. "Are you? That's funny."

Ashton watched for the next move, but the subject seemed in no way to interest Ford. Instead of following it up he began afresh.

"Have you any money lying idle?" he asked abruptly. "About a thousand pounds."

Ashton recognized that the mysterious stranger was about to disclose both himself and whatever object he had in seeking him out. He cast a quick glance about him.

"I can always find money," he said guardedly. "What's the proposition?"

With pretended nervousness Ford leaned forward and began the story he had rehearsed. It was a new version of an old swindle and to every self-respecting confidence man was well known as the "sick engineer" game. The plot is very simple. The sick engineer is supposed to be a mining engineer who, as an expert, has examined a gold mine and reported against it. For his services the company paid him partly in stock. He falls ill and is at the point of death. While he has been ill much gold has been found in the mine he examined, and the stock which he considers worthless is now valuable. Of this, owing to his illness, he is ignorant. One confidence man acts the part of the sick engineer, and the other that of a broker who knows the engineer possesses the stock but has no money with which to purchase it from him. For a share of the stock he offers to tell the dupe where it and the engineer can be found. They visit the man, apparently at the point of death, and the dupe gives him money for his stock. Later the dupe finds the stock is worthless, and the supposed engineer and the supposed broker divide the money he paid for it. In telling the story Ford pretended he was the broker and that he thought in Ashton he had found a dupe who would buy the stock from the sick engineer.

As the story unfolded and Ashton appreciated the part Ford expected him to play in it, his emotions were so varied that he was in danger of apoplexy. Amusement, joy, chagrin, and indignation illuminated his countenance. His cigar ceased to burn, and with his eyes opened wide he regarded Ford in pitying wonder.

"Wait!" he commanded. He shook his head uncomprehendingly. "Tell me," he asked, "do I look as easy as that, or are you just naturally foolish?"

Ford pretended to fall into a state of great alarm.

"I don't understand," he stammered.

"Why, son," exclaimed Ashton kindly, "I was taught that story in the public schools. I invented it. I stopped using it before you cut your teeth. Gee!" he exclaimed delightedly. "I knew I had grown respectable-looking, but I didn't think I was so damned respectable-looking as that!" He began to laugh silently; so greatly was he amused that the tears shone in his eyes and his shoulders shook.

"I'm sorry for you, son," he protested, "but that's the funniest thing that's come my way in two years. And you buying me hot-house grapes, too, and fancy water! I wish you could see your face," he taunted.

Ford pretended to be greatly chagrined.

"All right," he declared roughly. "The laugh's on me this time, but just because I lost one trick, don't think I don't know my business. Now that I'm wise to what YOU are we can work together and—"

The face of young Mr. Ashton became instantly grave. His jaws snapped like a trap. When he spoke his tone was assured and slightly contemptuous.

"Not with ME you can't work!" he said.

"Don't think because I fell down on this," Ford began hotly.

"I'm not thinking of you at all," said Ashton. "You're a nice little fellow all right, but you have sized me up wrong. I am on the 'straight and narrow' that leads back to little old New York and God's country, and I am warranted not to run off my trolley."

The words were in the vernacular, but the tone in which the young man spoke rang so confidently that it brought to Ford a pleasant thrill of satisfaction. From the first he had found in the personality of the young man something winning and likable; a shrewd manliness and tolerant good-humor. His eyes may have shown his sympathy, for, in sudden confidence, Ashton leaned nearer.

"It's like this," he said. "Several years ago I made a bad break and, about a year later, they got on to me and I had to cut and run. In a month the law of limitation lets me loose and I can go back. And you can bet I'm GOING back. I will be on the bowsprit of the first boat. I've had all I want of the 'fugitive-from-justice' game, thank you, and I have taken good care to keep a clean bill of health so that I won't have to play it again. They've been trying to get me for several years—especially the Pinkertons. They have chased me all over Europe. Chased me with all kinds of men; sometimes with women; they've tried everything except bloodhounds. At first I thought YOU were a 'Pink,' that's why—"

"I!" interrupted Ford, exploding derisively. "That's GOOD! That's one on YOU." He ceased laughing and regarded Ashton kindly. "How do you know I'm not?" he asked.

For an instant the face of the bookmaker grew a shade less red and his eyes searched those of Ford in a quick agony of suspicion. Ford continued to smile steadily at him, and Ashton breathed with relief.

"I'll take a chance with you," he said, "and if you are as bad a detective as you are a sport I needn't worry."

They both laughed, and, with sudden mutual liking, each raised his glass and nodded.

"But they haven't got me yet," continued Ashton, "and unless they get me in the next thirty days I'm free. So you needn't think that I'll help you. It's 'never again' for me. The first time, that was the fault of the crowd I ran with; the second time, that would be MY fault. And there ain't going to be any second time."

He shook his head doggedly, and with squared shoulders leaned back in his chair.

"If it only breaks right for me," he declared, "I'll settle down in one of those 'Own-your own-homes,' forty-five minutes from Broadway, and never leave the wife and the baby."

The words almost brought Ford to his feet. He had forgotten the wife and the baby. He endeavored to explain his surprise by a sudden assumption of incredulity.

"Fancy you married!" he exclaimed.

"Married!" protested Ashton. "I'm married to the finest little lady that ever wore skirts, and in thirty-seven days I'll see her again. Thirty-seven days," he repeated impatiently. "Gee! That's a hell of a long time!"

Ford studied the young man with increased interest. That he was speaking sincerely, from the heart, there seemed no possible doubt.

Ashton frowned and his face clouded. "I've not been able to treat her just right," he volunteered. "If she wrote me, the letters might give them a clew, and I don't write HER because I don't want her to know all my troubles until they're over. But I know," he added, "that five minutes' talk will set it all right. That is, if she still feels about me the way I feel about her."

The man crushed his cigar in his fingers and threw the pieces on the floor. "That's what's been the worst!" he exclaimed bitterly. "Not hearing, not knowing. It's been hell!"

His eyes as he raised them were filled with suffering, deep and genuine.

Ford rose suddenly. "Let's go down to the Savoy for supper," he said.

"Supper!" growled Ashton. "What's the use of supper? Do you suppose cold chicken and a sardine can keep me from THINKING?"

Ford placed his hand on the other's shoulder.

"You come with me," he said kindly. "I'm going to do you a favor. I'm going to bring you a piece of luck. Don't ask me any questions," he commanded hurriedly. "Just take my word for it."

They had sat so late over their cigars that when they reached the restaurant on the Embankment the supper-room was already partly filled, and the corridors and lounge were brilliantly lit and gay with well-dressed women. Ashton regarded the scene with gloomy eyes. Since he had spoken of his wife he had remained silent, chewing savagely on a fresh cigar. But Ford was grandly excited. He did not know exactly what he intended to do. He was prepared to let events direct themselves, but of two things he was assured: Mrs. Ashton loved her husband, and her husband loved her. As the god in the car who was to bring them together, he felt a delightful responsibility.

The young men left the coat-room and came down the short flight of steps that leads to the wide lounge of the restaurant. Ford slightly in advance, searching with his eyes for Mrs Ashton, found her seated alone in the lounge, evidently waiting for him. At the first glance she was hardly be recognized. Her low-cut dinner gown of black satin that clung to her like a wet bath robe was the last word of the new fashion; and since Ford had seen her her blond hair had been arranged by an artist. Her appearance was smart, elegant, daring. She was easily the prettiest and most striking-looking woman in the room, and for an instant Ford stood gazing at her, trying to find in the self-possessed young woman the deserted wife of the steamer. She did not see Ford. Her eyes were following the progress down the hall of a woman, and her profile was toward him.

The thought of the happiness he was about to bring to two young people gave Ford the sense of a genuine triumph, and when he turned to Ashton to point out his wife to him he was thrilling with pride and satisfaction. His triumph received a bewildering shock. Already Ashton had discovered the presence of Mrs. Ashton. He was standing transfixed, lost to his surroundings, devouring her with his eyes. And then, to the amazement of Ford, his eyes filled with fear, doubt, and anger. Swiftly, with the movement of a man ducking a blow, he turned and sprang up the stairs and into the coatroom. Ford, bewildered and more conscious of his surroundings, followed him less quickly, and was in consequence only in time to see Ashton, dragging his overcoat behind him, disappear into the court-yard. He seized his own coat and raced in pursuit. As he ran into the court-yard Ashton, in the Strand, was just closing the door of a taxicab, but before the chauffeur could free it from the surrounding traffic, Ford had dragged the door open, and leaped inside. Ashton was huddled in the corner, panting, his face pale with alarm.

"What the devil ails you?" roared Ford. "Are you trying to shake me? You've got to come back. You must speak to her."

"Speak to her!" repeated Ashton. His voice was sunk to a whisper. The look of alarm in his face was confused with one grim and menacing. "Did you know she was there?" he demanded softly. "Did you take me there, knowing—?"

"Of course I knew," protested Ford. "She's been looking for you—"

His voice subsided in a squeak of amazement and pain. Ashton's left hand had shot out and swiftly seized his throat. With the other he pressed an automatic revolver against Ford's shirt front.

"I know she's been looking for me," the man whispered thickly. "For two years she's been looking for me. I know all about HER! But, WHO IN HELL ARE YOU?"

Ford, gasping and gurgling, protested loyally.

"You are wrong!" he cried. "She's been at home waiting for you. She thinks you have deserted her and your baby. I tell you she loves you, you fool, she LOVES you!"

The fingers on his throat suddenly relaxed; the flaming eyes of Ashton, glaring into his, wavered and grew wide with amazement.

"Loves me," he whispered. "WHO loves me?"

"Your wife," protested Ford; "the girl at the Savoy, your wife."

Again the fingers of Ashton pressed deep around his neck.

"That is not my wife," he whispered. His voice was unpleasantly cold and grim. "That's 'Baby Belle,' with her hair dyed, a detective lady of the Pinkertons, hired to find me. And YOU know it. Now, who are YOU?"

To permit him to reply Ashton released his hand, but at the same moment, in a sudden access of fear, dug the revolver deeper into the pit of Ford's stomach.

"Quick!" he commanded. "Never mind the girl. WHO ARE YOU?"

Ford collapsed against the cushioned corner of the cab. "And she begged me to find you," he roared, "because she LOVED you, because she wanted to BELIEVE in you!" He held his arms above his head. "Go ahead and shoot!" he cried. "You want to know who I am?" he demanded. His voice rang with rage. "I'm an amateur. Just a natural born fool-amateur! Go on and shoot!"

The gun in Ashton's hand sank to his knee. Between doubt and laughter his face was twisted in strange lines. The cab was whirling through a narrow, unlit street leading to Covent Garden. Opening the door Ashton called to the chauffeur, and then turned to Ford.

"You get off here!" he commanded. "Maybe you're a 'Pink,' maybe you're a good fellow. I think you're a good fellow, but I'm not taking any chances. Get out!"

Ford scrambled to the street, and as the taxicab again butted itself forward, Ashton leaned far through the window. "Good-by, son," he called. "Send me a picture-postal card to Paris. For I am off to Maxim's," he cried, "and you can go to—"

"Not at all!" shouted the amateur detective indignantly. "I'm going back to take supper with 'Baby Belle'!"